JOCASTA CARR
Movie Star

— Roy Gerrard —

Farrar, Straus & Giroux
New York

When young Jocasta reached her teens
    Both she and Belle were movie queens,
Whose audiences held their breath
    As dog and damsel diced with death,
And faithful fans were thrilled to see
    How Belle could set her mistress free.

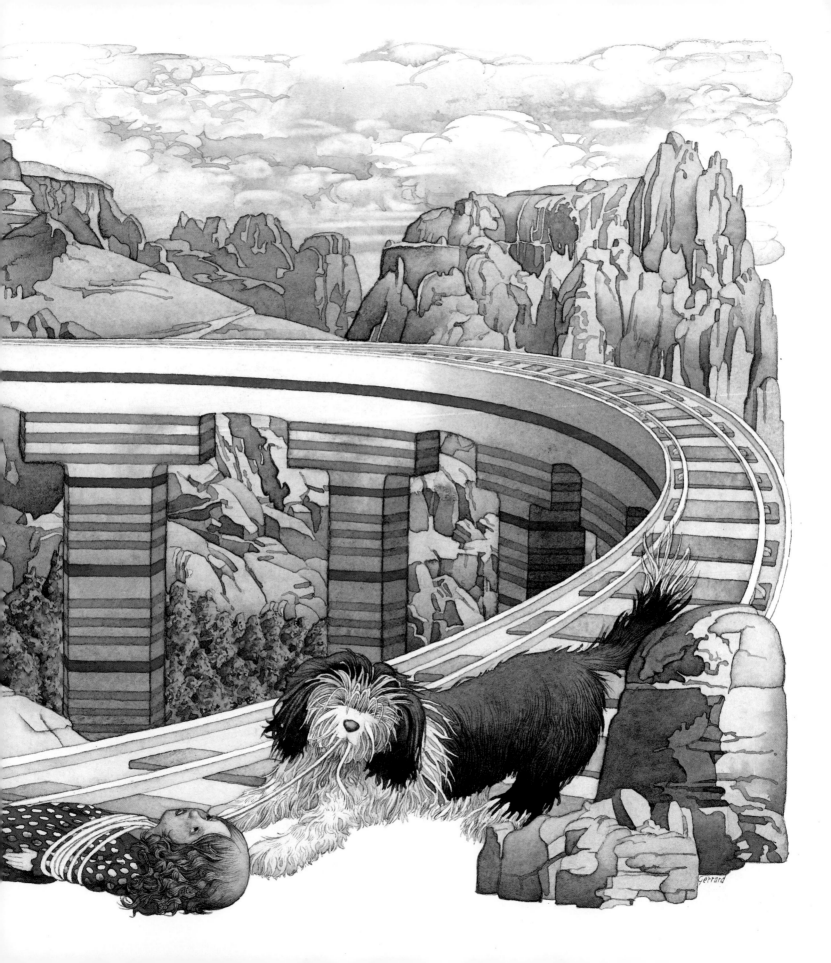

On weekend breaks they loved to fly
   Their scarlet seaplane through the sky,
Or, when the days were not too cool,
   They stayed relaxing by their pool.

The film producer Maxwell Pym
    Was keen that Belle should work for him;
He tried to make Jocasta sell,
    But she refused to part with Belle.

Pym flew into a fearful rage
  And threatened Jo, but at this stage
Belle leapt and gave him such a bite
  The villain turned and fled in fright.

Then Maxwell Pym, that wicked man,
Devised a subtle, secret plan:
By tempting Belle with meat, he got
    The dog to come aboard his yacht.
Too late she saw his trickery —
    They'd captured her and put to sea!

Jocasta sorely missed her friend,
    She searched the town for weeks on end,
Informed the police and advertised,
    Till in the end she realized
That Maxwell Pym, the ne'er-do-well,
    Must be the one who'd kidnapped Belle.

Jo phoned around and soon heard talk
    That Pym and Co. were in New York,
But after flying there she found
    Them rumored to be London-bound,
So, climbing back into her plane,
    She flew in hot pursuit again.

Jo's fearless transatlantic flight
　　Took two whole days and one whole night,
And though her London fans were glad
　　To see her, yet their news looked bad,
For Maxwell and his ghastly crew
　　Had sailed instead to Wangaloo.

Jocasta wondered what to do —
   She'd never heard of Wangaloo —
But then she met a friendly chap
   Who helped her find it on the map,
And Wangaloo turned out to be
   An island in the Java Sea.

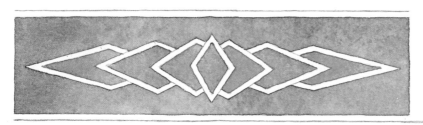

Undaunted by her friends, who said
   She'd end up either lost or dead,
Jo packed her suitcase and resolved
   (Despite the distances involved)
To carry on and see it through,
   Then — 'Chocks away' for Wangaloo.

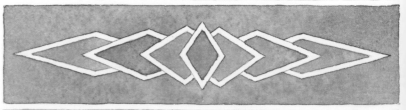

Through stormy clouds and driving rain
  Jo piloted her sturdy plane;
In Paris, Rome, and Istanbul
  She stopped, but, once her tanks were full,
Flew off again, mile after mile,
  Toward the far-flung tropic isle.

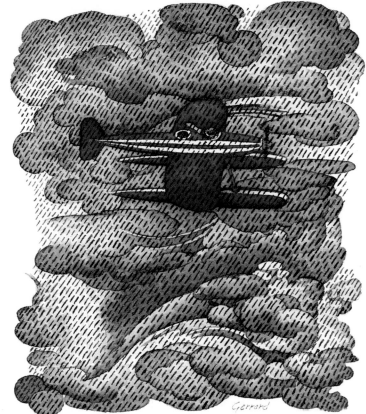

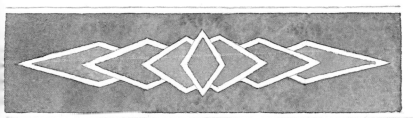

As she passed by a rocky peak,
  The radiator sprang a leak!
She barely missed the mountaintop
  But, knowing she would have to stop,
Jo safely brought her plane to land
  In barren wastes of burning sand.

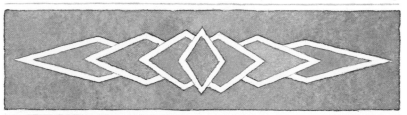

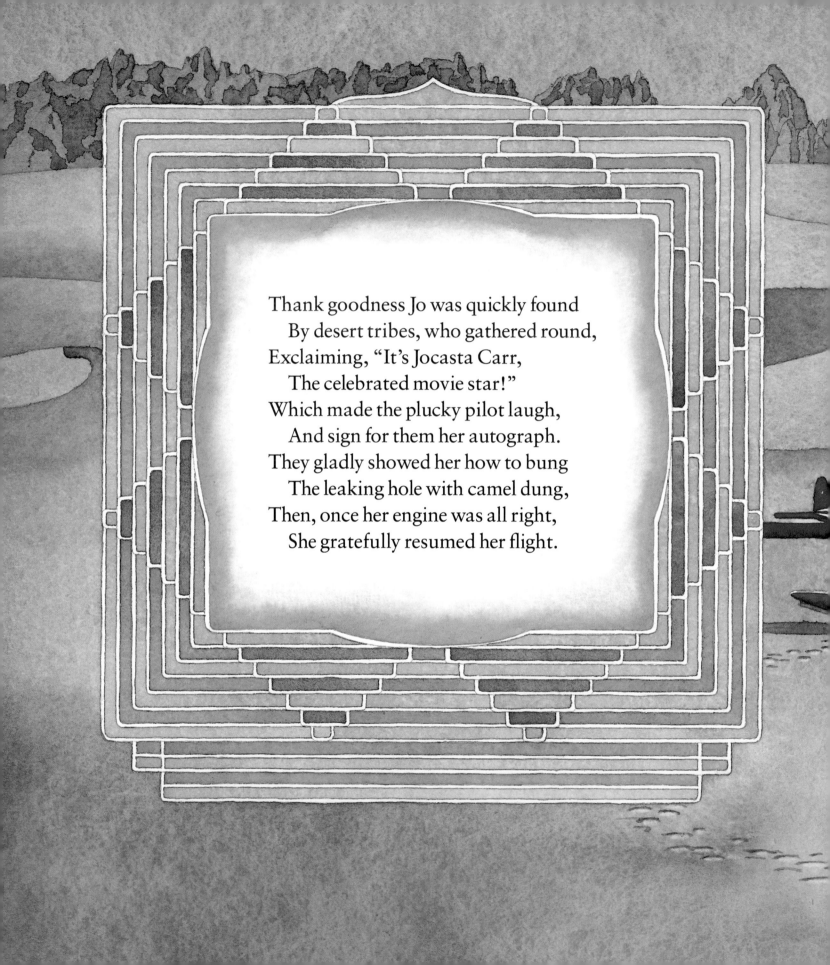

Thank goodness Jo was quickly found
   By desert tribes, who gathered round,
Exclaiming, "It's Jocasta Carr,
   The celebrated movie star!"
Which made the plucky pilot laugh,
   And sign for them her autograph.
They gladly showed her how to bung
   The leaking hole with camel dung,
Then, once her engine was all right,
   She gratefully resumed her flight.

In India, completely lost,
　　With miles of jungle to be crossed,
Jo landed in a likely place
　　But trembled when she turned to face
A tiger of stupendous size,
　　Who looked at her with hungry eyes.

No need for Jo to get upset —
  The tiger was a playful pet,
Whose master, stepping into view,
  Gave Jo a cheerful "How d'you do?"
Her newfound friend was, furthermore,
  The wealthy Rajah of Mysore.

This odd, eccentric gentleman
    Was quite by chance Jo's greatest fan.
Enchanted by his favorite star,
    He towed her home behind his car
And helped Jocasta to unwind.
    (He really was extremely kind.)

Jo's final journey proved to be
Across a shark-infested sea;
Down to the waves, her fuel all spent,
She made a perilous descent,
But help was near — to her delight
A ship came steaming into sight.

The captain soon took Jo on board
  And fortunately could afford
Enough spare fuel to fill her tanks,
  So she, with gratitude and thanks,
Took off again into the blue
  And came at last to Wangaloo.

She landed with a gentle glide,
  To find Pym's yacht unoccupied.
Jo weighed the anchor with much glee
  And watched the yacht drift out to sea,
Then stole ashore while Maxwell slept
  And found the cage where Belle was kept.

So overjoyed was Belle to see
   Her mistress come to set her free,
She hurtled into Jo's embrace,
   She nuzzled her and licked her face,
And then they tiptoed down the beach
   To fly away beyond Pym's reach.

Awakened by the engine's roar,
  The hoodwinked hoods rushed to the shore.
Too late to intercept the plane,
  They screamed and yelled, but all in vain.
Jo waved goodbye as off she flew,
  To leave them stuck on Wangaloo.

Abandoned to a cruel fate,
   Pym's gang was in a dreadful state,
For there, on lonely Wangaloo,
   The things they found to eat were few;
They stayed alive by eating meals
   Of slimy snails and slippery eels.

To Pym it seemed, as weeks dragged past,
That they were doomed — until, at last
(Tipped off by Jo), the police arrived
And found the gang had just survived;
Subdued and ragged, starved and frail,
They faced a lengthy stretch in jail.

So dognapping cost Maxwell dear
    And spelled the end of his career:
He, who'd known both power and riches,
    Faced a future digging ditches,
Whilst Jo and Belle once more became
    Secure in luxury and fame,
And both of them resumed with pride
    Their starring story, side by side.